PRESENTED TO:

_____

FROM:

_____

DATE:

_____

LULLABY PRAYER

Tamara Bundy

illustrated by
Jill Howarth

An Imprint of Thomas Nelson

Lullaby Prayer

© 2020 Tamara Bundy

Tommy Nelson, PO Box 141000, Nashville, TN 37214

Published in Nashville, Tennessee, by Tommy Nelson. Tommy Nelson is an imprint of Thomas Nelson. Thomas Nelson is a registered trademark of HarperCollins Christian Publishing, Inc.

Tommy Nelson titles may be purchased in bulk for educational, business, fundraising, or sales promotional use. For information, please e-mail SpecialMarkets@ ThomasNelson.com.

Illustrated by Jill Howarth.

Library of Congress Cataloging-in-Publication Data

Names: Bundy, Tamara, author. | Howarth, Jill, illustrator.
Title: Lullaby prayer / Tamara Bundy.
Description: Nashville, TN : Thomas Nelson, 2020. | Audience: Ages 4-8 |
Summary: "With its gentle depictions of a peaceful countryside slipping into sleep, this dreamy picture book from author Tamara Bundy and illustrator Jill Howarth reminds children that God is with them the whole night through"-- Provided by publisher.
Identifiers: LCCN 2020015580 (print) | LCCN 2020015581 (ebook) | ISBN 9781400221479 (hardcover) | ISBN 9781400221486 (epub)
Subjects: LCSH: Bedtime prayers--Juvenile literature.
Classification: LCC BV283.B43 B86 2020 (print) | LCC BV283.B43 (ebook) | DDC 242/.82--dc23
LC record available at https://lccn.loc.gov/2020015580
LC ebook record available at https://lccn.loc.gov/2020015581

Printed in Korea

20 21 22 23 24 IMG 10 9 8 7 6 5 4 3 2 1

Mfr: IMG / Paju, Songunsa, Korea / October 2020 / PO #9589868

To Vivi:
*Mimi loves you more than
even these words can say.*

When cool darkness

unfolds her blanket,

gently *draping* the edge of the day,

and the tired lawn lets loose a *yawn*,

**May God's peace cover
you as we pray.**

When the moon smiles over the farmland,

nestling its beams in the cradle of night,

and peeking stars wink and blink *hello,*

**May God guard you with
His perfect sight.**

When fireflies speckle the sky,

like *ballerinas* against golden moonbeams,

as they *waltz* with bats

gobbling up gnats,

**May God's joy dance
through all your dreams.**

When the whip-poor-will's lullabies *echo*

with its whistles and warbles so blue,

and the *hooting owl* croons from his bough,

May God sing a
good-night song for you.

When the willow tree stretches her limbs

and *weaves* her fingers through ribbons of air

in hopes of catching a bright tumbling star,

**May God's arms gather
you in His care.**

When masked raccoons
wake, creep, and *climb*

from the hollow

of their old oak tree,

sneaking through fields and finding their feast,

May you know God gives more than we see.

When the barn's drumming doors start tapping

to the beat of wind's *whispering song*

while safe walls hide the animals inside,

May God's shelter surround you, tall and strong.

When mama cow comforts her calf
with a lullaby, *hummed* in the hay,
and *moooos* and *kisses*
with sweet-clover *wishes*,

**May our Father calm
your cares away.**

When clouds describe their
great adventures

and all they've seen
while they drift,

as they *chatter* and *splatter*
on the windowpane,

**May you thank God
for all today's gifts.**

When the thirsty ground *gulps* up the rain
and drinking daisies *sway* in delight

while seeds *snooze* below

so they can grow,

**May God's rest restore
you in the night.**

When your night-light
invites the darkness

to make *glad shadows*
play on your wall

as soft beams shimmer, glisten, and glimmer,

**May God's light
guide you above all.**

When your sleepy, sweet puppy cuddles close,

a warm friend for all the night through,

remember, God loves all—both *big* and *small*.

May you know just how
much He loves you.

When your tired head sinks into pillowy fluff

and sweet visions *float* into view,

with a world of possibilities waiting,

May God help your best dreams come true.

When the warmth of your blanket hugs you,
and it's time for one last
good-night kiss,

know *I will be near* and *God is right here.*

May He bless us with more nights like this.